Daniel San Souci

TRICYCLE PRESS
Berkeley / Toronto

A Clubhouse Book

Tricycle Press
an imprint of Ten Speed Press
PO Box 7123
Berkeley, California 94707
www.tricyclepress.com

Design by Tasha Hall based on a previous design by Toni Tajima and Daniel San Souci
Typeset in Stinky Butt

Library of Congress Cataloging-in-Publication Data
San Souci, Daniel.
   The Mighty Pigeon Club / by Daniel San Souci.
      p. cm.
   Summary: When some homing pigeons need a new home, a group of friends take them
and start the "Mighty Pigeon Club," only to find that they have taken on more than they
bargained for.
   ISBN-13: 978-1-58246-213-4
   ISBN-10: 1-58246-213-5
[1. Homing pigeons—Fiction. 2. Pigeons—Fiction. 3. Clubs—Fiction.] I. Title.
   PZ7.S1946Mi 2007
   [E]—dc22
                                     2006037073

First Tricycle Press printing, 2007
Printed in Singapore
1 2 3 4 5 6 – 11 10 09 08 07

For my sister
Ellen May—
best sister in the world

On Saturday afternoon we met at the clubhouse. We could see Arthur Gizeinski's pigeons flying high in the sky. The birds dove, tumbled, and rolled.

"It would be *so* cool if we were pigeons," said my older brother, Bobby.

"It would be like riding a roller coaster you never had to get off," said Allison.

"Yeah," said my younger brother, Mike. "Pigeons have it made!"

Arthur was one of the presenters at the next school assembly. He gave a talk about homing pigeons.

He showed lots of pictures and held up a pigeon he made out of modeling clay.

"Pigeons are war heroes. They deliver messages during battles and are used in sea rescues," said Arthur. "But the best thing is that they can find their way home from hundreds of miles away."

After Arthur's talk, we started going over to his house after school.

He liked to watch his pigeons do their tricks. Then he'd time how fast they flew.

One day, Arthur didn't show up at school. On our way home we stopped by his house.
His mother answered the door.

"Arthur feels terrible," she said. "We just found out that he is allergic to bird feathers."
"I hope he gets better real soon," I said.

"Would you kids be interested in Arthur's birds? We have to find a new home for them."
We couldn't believe what we were hearing.
"Sure . . . we'll take them," said Bobby.

We were so happy we danced all the way home.

With some chicken wire and scrap wood we turned the clubhouse into a pigeon coop.

The next day we filled it with pigeons and became "The Mighty Pigeon Club."

Soon, Mom got a phone call from our neighbor, Mrs. Crenshaw.

"What is all that strange noise coming from your backyard?" she wanted to know.

We were called in to explain why the clubhouse was full of pigeons.

Bobby's speech about how pigeons save lives and are war heroes didn't impress Mom and Dad, so he tried to convince them another way.

"Please, please," he begged. "You'll never even know they're here . . . we promise . . . oh, come on, pleeease . . . let us keep them."

"Okay," Mom said. "As long as you take excellent care of them."

"We'll be watching closely," said Dad.

To make sure the pigeons would return after we let them fly, Arthur told us to keep them in the clubhouse for ten days. So we just imagined what we would do with them.

"There must be all kinds of contests we could enter them in," said Allison.
"I bet we'd win huge trophies," said Bobby.
"And cash prizes, too," said Mike.

But after just a few days we discovered a big problem. "Quick!" said Craig. "We've got to get our stuff out of the clubhouse. The pigeons are pooping on everything!"

"How can a few birds make such a big mess?" asked
Andy. "They're pooping machines."

"Somebody can be the official Clubhouse cleaner," said
Bobby, "and whoever it is, won't have to pay club dues."

There were no takers.

"Okay," said Bobby, "then we'll all take turns.
Youngest goes first and oldest goes last."
    Everyone thought this was a good idea except Mike,
who was the youngest. We voted and he lost.
    So that afternoon Mike loaded up a shopping bag
with pigeon poop.

The ten days finally ended, and we let the pigeons fly. At first they fluttered out the door and landed on the clubhouse roof. But then the mighty pigeons took off and shot upward, like a squadron of fighter planes.

We clapped and hollered as they dove, tumbled, and
rolled. The pigeons circled the block and landed back on
the roof. Then, one by one, they entered the clubhouse
through the hatch above the window.

Every day we'd meet to watch the pigeons fly.
But soon complaints started coming from the neighbors.

"Those pigeons poop on my laundry," said Mrs. Crenshaw.

Professor Stern said that the pigeons landed on his windowsills and peeked inside his house. "I have no privacy anymore."

Mrs. Turnipseed said that one of the pigeons flew inside her bathroom and landed on the tub. "That bird acted like it owned the place."

Mrs. Gray was painting a watercolor of her garden when one of the pigeons flew by. "It pooped all over the painting, ruining it beyond repair," she said.

But by far the angriest neighbor was Mr. Turnipseed. His TV antenna became a favorite spot for the pigeons to gather. "Every time those birds are up there, the screen is full of wavy lines," he fumed.

"You're going to have to do something about those birds," said Dad.

"The way things are going, the neighbors are going to stop talking to us," said Mom.

Billy came up with an idea. His father, who was a big football fan, had an air horn that he blew during games.

"When the pigeons land somewhere we don't want them to, we'll just blast the horn and they'll leave," said Billy.

The next day, Billy climbed over Mrs. Crenshaw's fence and blasted the horn. The sound was earsplitting. The pigeons flew up in the air and hovered for a short time, then landed back on the clothesline.

"Out of my backyard, mister!" screamed Mrs. Crenshaw.
Billy leaped over the fence and handed the air horn to Bobby. "Next time, *you* do it," he said.
Bobby handed it back to him. "This isn't going to work."

As the days went by, not only did the neighbors keep complaining, but we were starting to become bored. We spent most of our time scraping pigeon poop and listening to Mom and Dad remind us of our "pigeon duties."

When Bobby said, "I think we should find another home for the pigeons," we all agreed.

On Saturday we set up a stand in front of our house offering "free pigeons." Lots of cars drove by. Some people honked and waved, but no one stopped.

Then the answer came to us by accident.
On our way to the park, we passed by old
St. Francis Church.

"Look," said Mike. "Tons of pigeons!"

"And there's even a statue of a saint blessing them!" said Allison.

"This is the perfect place to let our pigeons go," said Bobby.

"It's pigeon heaven," I added.

"But won't they just fly back the clubhouse?" asked Craig.

"Are you kidding?" said Bobby. "Once they get a taste of this place they'll never want to leave."

We went back to the clubhouse, loaded the pigeons in boxes, and returned to the church.

When we opened the boxes, our pigeons flew up to the church roof and started mixing with the other birds.

Just then, a window in the church flew open and a man yelled, "What are you hooligans doing?"

"Giving you more pigeons," said Andy.

"Well, I don't want the ones that are here, let alone yours," he said. "I'm coming right down, and we'll see what your parents have to say about all this!"

"Ditch!" yelled Bobby, and we dropped the empty boxes and raced the entire way home.

By the time we reached the clubhouse, we found all our pigeons waiting for us. And they had brought along some friends from St. Francis Church.

"Hey look," said Allison. "One of the church birds has a band on its leg with a telephone number."

When Bobby called the number, an older kid named Marvin answered the phone. He was happy we had found his missing pigeon, and we offered to take it to him.

Marvin met us in his front yard and thanked us for
returning his pigeon.

"You sure like birds," I said.

"Someday I'm going to be an ornithologist," he said.
"That's a bird scientist."

In his backyard he had two big aviaries. One held canaries and the other was full of pigeons.

"About a month ago I almost got a bunch of free pigeons from an allergic Kid," he said. "But just before I got there, his mother gave them to somebody else."

That day, Marvin got the pigeons he wanted, and we got our clubhouse back.